Puss in Boots

Anne Cassidy and Roger Fereday

W

1
The Miller's Sad Son

The miller's son was very poor. "I have
no money!" he said. "I even have patches
on my clothes."

"Don't be sad," said Puss. "You have me
– a talking cat."

"My older brothers have more than me.
What can I do?"

"You can trust me," said Puss.

Puss was a very
clever cat.

"I have a splendid plan," said Puss. "I will make you richer than your brothers. I just need a bag and some boots!"

The miller's son was pleased. He longed to be rich. He gave Puss the boots and bag.

"What's your plan?" he said.

"Do you trust me?" Puss asked.

The miller's son nodded.

"Will you do everything I say?"

"Yes, yes, yes!"

"I'll call you the Marquis of Carabas and very soon all your dreams will come true."

Puss went out into the woods. He used
the bag to make a trap to catch a rabbit.
He waited and waited. Then a rabbit came
along and he caught it.
"I'll take this rabbit to the royal palace."

"Your Majesty," said Puss, "I bring you the gift of this beautiful rabbit. It comes from my master, the splendid Marquis of Carabas." The king and the princess were very pleased.

2
The King and the Princess

Puss took lots of gifts to the palace.
"Your Majesty, my master, the Marquis of
Carabas, sends you these gifts."

The ladies and gentlemen at court were
amazed. The king was delighted.
"I would very much like to meet the
Marquis of Carabas," the princess said,
smiling. This was just what Puss
had hoped for!

One day, the king and princess went out in their carriage. Puss's splendid plan reached the next stage.

"Quick," Puss said to his master, "take off your clothes and get into the river."

The miller's son took off his clothes and jumped in. Then Puss hid the clothes under a bush.

"Stay in the water," Puss whispered, "and do everything I say."

The miller's son splashed around in the river. The king and princess drove up.

"Help!" cried Puss, as loud as he could.
"Help!"

The king and princess stopped their
carriage. "A robber has taken the Marquis
of Carabas's clothes and pushed him into
the river!" cried Puss.

"That's terrible," said the king.

"I think he's drowning," said Puss.

The king's servant saved the miller's son and gave him some clothes.

The princess smiled sweetly at him.

"Thank you for your gifts, Marquis," she said.

3
The Ogre's Castle

The king and the princess
offered to take their new friend back to his
castle. They waited for him in their carriage.
"What am I going to do?" the miller's son
said. "I have no castle. I'm not really the
Marquis of Carabas. Now they will know
that I am an imposter!"

"Don't worry," said Puss, "I have a splendid plan, remember! You go with the king and princess and I will run ahead. Follow me and you will have a castle."

Puss ran off as fast as he could.

Nearby was a beautiful castle, home to a terrible ogre. Everyone was afraid of him. Puss did not care. He was going to trick the ogre out of his castle.

He went to find the ogre's servants.

"Soon the king will arrive in his carriage. You must tell him that this castle belongs to the Marquis of Carabas."

The servants were quiet.

"This is your chance to get rid of that terrible ogre!" Puss declared.

The king rode by. "Who owns these pretty woods and fields?" he asked.

"The Marquis of Carabas," came the reply from the ogre's servants.

"And what about that beautiful castle over there?" asked the princess.

The miller's son gave a tiny smile. The ogre's servants looked at the castle.

"Why, the Marquis of Carabas owns it!" they said.

19

4
The Ogre's Magic Tricks

Puss ran ahead to the castle. He opened the big wooden door and went inside to look for the ogre. Puss found him sitting in a chair. He had very hairy eyebrows and a red nose. "Who are you?" the ogre said, angrily.

"I am Puss."

The ogre was surprised to see a talking cat.

"People say you have magical powers.

I have come here to see if that is true!"

said Puss.

"It is TRUE!" the ogre shouted.

"But can you turn into a lion?" said Puss.

The ogre instantly turned himself into
a giant lion with big claws. Puss nearly
jumped out of his boots! Then
the ogre roared and Puss
was scared.

"That's very good," said Puss, quickly, "but I bet you can't turn yourself into something very small, like a tiny mouse!"

In a flash, the ogre turned into a tiny mouse. Puss smiled to himself. He was feeling quite hungry, so he gobbled the mouse up. Now the ogre was gone for good.

5
The Princess and the Miller's Son

Soon the king's carriage arrived at the castle.

Puss was there to greet everyone.

"This truly is a fine castle," the princess said.

"I'm glad you like it, Your Majesty," said Puss.
"The Marquis of Carabas is very proud of it."
The miller's son tried not to look too surprised.
"Maybe the Marquis of Carabas needs a wife
to help him look after it," said the princess.
The miller's son smiled.

The princess and the miller's son soon got married. Everyone was invited and there were loud cheers from the crowd.

Puss in Boots was pleased.

His splendid plan had worked.

Now he could live happily ever after!

About the story

Puss in Boots is a European fairy tale. The oldest written version dates from the Italian author Giovanni Francesco Straparola, from around 1550 CE, although the cat in his story is really a fairy and the ogre is really a lord. Charles Perrault also includes a version of the story in his collection of fairy tales from 1697. The story could be linked to far older Indian folk tales that also feature a cat who uses trickery to his advantage. This trickster cat is a popular character to this day, and featured in an animated film *Puss in Boots* from Dreamworks in 2011, with Antonio Banderas taking up the speaking cat role he played in the *Shrek* films.

Be in the story!

Imagine you are the miller's son. Will you tell the princess about Puss's clever plan? How do you think she will feel?

Now imagine you are Puss. How do you feel when your plan comes together?

Franklin Watts
First published in Great Britain in 2016 by The Watts Publishing Group

Series Editor: Jackie Hamley
Series Advisor: Catherine Glavina
Series Designer: Cathryn Gilbert

A CIP catalogue record for this book is available
from the British Library.

The artwork for this story first appeared in
Leapfrog Fairy Tales: Puss in Boots

ISBN 978 1 4451 4669 0 (hbk)
ISBN 978 1 4451 4670 6 (library ebook)
ISBN 978 1 4451 4671 3 (pbk)

Printed in China

Franklin Watts
An imprint of
Hachette Children's Group
Part of The Watts Publishing Group
Carmelite House
50 Victoria Embankment
London EC4Y 0DZ

An Hachette UK Company
www.hachette.co.uk

www.franklinwatts.co.uk

FSC
www.fsc.org
MIX
Paper from
responsible sources
FSC® C104740